This Little Tiger book belongs to:

_____

_____

_____

For my parents, with love and gratitude,
and for my ever-creative muse
~ P. B.

For Minnie, Harry and Geri
~ G. P.-R.

LITTLE TIGER PRESS LTD,
an imprint of the Little Tiger Group
1 Coda Studios, 189 Munster Road, London SW6 6AW
www.littletiger.co.uk

First published in Great Britain 2003
This edition published 2018

Printed in China • LTP/1800/2262/0418

2 4 6 8 10 9 7 5 3

birds were chirping,

and a million insects were
humming and buzzing.
What a lot of noise!

It was time for
Baby Leo to have his morning nap.
"He'll never get to sleep with all this noise,"
said Mama Lion to Leo's father.
"Isn't there something you can do?"

"Do?" said Papa Lion. "Do? I am king of all the animals. Of course there is something I can do!" He stood up tall, puffed out his huge chest, and roared . . .

And so, Baby Leo fell asleep. Then Papa Lion
whispered softly, but clearly so that
all the creatures could hear him:

"If any of you makes a noise,
and wakes up Leo, I will gobble you up."

All was quiet in the jungle.
Quiet as the morning mist.
Quiet as the opening flowers.
Quiet as a baby sleeping.
Suddenly . . .

Cawing and crowing, squeaking and squawking.
Beaks pecking and claws scratching.
Two parrots were arguing in the bushes!

"**Quiet!**" said Papa Lion, as loud as he dared,
in case Baby Leo was still sleeping.
"It's all right," said Mama Lion. "Leo's fast asleep."
"Oh, well," said Papa Lion. "But I would have liked a snack."

Once again, all was quiet in the jungle.
Quiet as the trees growing up to the sky.
Quiet as the leaves reaching up to the light.
Quiet as a baby sleeping. Suddenly . . .

Chuckling
and chortling,

sniggering
and snickering.

The hyena was laughing.
Laughing like hyenas do.

But nobody knew what was so funny.

"**Quiet!**" said Papa Lion, as loud as he dared,
in case his son was still sleeping.
"It's all right," said Mama Lion. "He's still asleep."
"Oh, well," said Papa Lion. "But I'm getting hungry."

Then all was quiet in the jungle.
Quiet as the calm after a storm.
Quiet as sunshine after rain.
Quiet as a baby sleeping. Suddenly . . .

Howling and hooting, screeching and chattering.
Swinging and swooping. A family of monkeys was
leaping through the trees!

"**Quiet!**" said Papa Lion, as loud as he dared,
just in case Leo was still sleeping.
"It's all right," said Mama Lion. "Leo's asleep."
"Oh, well," said Papa Lion. "But now I'm *very* hungry."

It was the middle of the day
and the jungle was hot and humid.
The animals crept into the shade
of the trees, drowsy and dozing.

And all was quiet in the jungle.
Quiet as the blazing sun.
Quiet as the shadows underneath the trees.
Quiet as a baby sleeping. Suddenly . . .

Splashing and squelching.

Oohing and aahing.

A hippopotamus was yawning in the cool, muddy shallows of the river.

"Quiet!" said Papa Lion, as loud as he dared,
in case the baby lion was still sleeping.
"It's all right," said Mama Lion. "Leo's fast asleep."
"Humph!" said Papa Lion.
"I guess my eyes are bigger than my belly."

But Papa Lion rubbed his tummy and began to think,
"I do wish someone would make just a little
more noise and wake up Baby Leo.
Just for a minute."

Yet all remained quiet in the jungle.
Quiet as a fish swimming in the river.
Quiet as a bird soaring in the sky.
Quiet as a baby sleeping. Suddenly . . .

A rumbling and growling,
a groaning and moaning, a gurgling and burbling.
A noise like nothing ever heard before!

Loud as thunder.
Loud as a banging drum.
Loud as a baby crying!

"It's me," said Papa Lion, meekly.
"My stomach is rumbling.
Because I'm so hungry!"